SABRINA THE TEENAGE WITCH: THE MAGIC WITHIN 3

Published by Archie Comic Publications, Inc.

325 Fayette Avenue, Mamaroneck, NY 10543-2318.

FIRST PRINTING.   PRINTED IN CANADA.

ISBN: 978-1-936975-60-0

PUBLISHER/CO-CEO:
Jonathan Goldwater
CO-CEO:
Nancy Silberkleit
PRESIDENT:
Mike Pellerito
CO-PRESIDENT/ EDITOR-IN-CHIEF:
Victor Gorelick
SENIOR VICE PRESIDENT, SALES & BUSINESS DEVELOPMENT:
Jim Sokolowski
SENIOR VICE PRESIDENT, PUBLISHING & OPERATIONS:
Harold Buchholz
VICE PRESIDENT, SPECIAL PROJECTS:
Steve Mooar

EXECUTIVE DIRECTOR OF EDITORIAL:
Paul Kaminski
PRODUCTION MANAGER:
Stephen Oswald
DIRECTOR OF PUBLICITY & MARKETING:
Steven Scott
PROJECT COORDINATOR/ BOOK DESIGN:
Duncan McLachlan
EDITORIAL ASSISTANT/ PROOFREADER:
Carly Inglis
PRODUCTION:
Kari Silbergleit

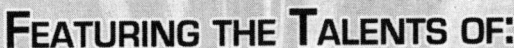

Featuring the Talents of:

STORY & PENCILS — Tania del Rio

INKS — Jim Amash

LETTERS — Teresa Davidson, John Workman, Phil Felix

COVER COLORS, RENDERING — Jason Jensen

Characters

SABRINA is still trying to be a normal teenager as much as she can in spite of spending most of her time in the Magic Realm. Her magical power is rapidly growing, and she's dating the young wizard Shinji, who knows a dangerous secret that could affect everyone in the Magic Realm.

The usually cool and laid-back **SHINJI** has started a new cause that could take the Magic Realm by storm . . . and his closest friends, including **LLANDRA** and Sabrina, have sworn to stand with him! Years ago, Shinji's parents were part of a political movement called *The Four Blades* who tried to wrest the Queen from her throne because they had learned a terrible secret about her. In the end, The Four Blades failed, but Shinji is determined to follow in their footsteps—especially since he thinks he knows the Queen's secret: the Mana Tree, the source of all magic and life in the Magic Realm, is dying, and the Queen is failing in her duty to keep it alive. To make things worse, monsters keep appearing and wreaking havoc, and a strange man by the name of Vosblanc seems to have some sort of control over them—and the Queen. Could he be behind all of the Magic Realm's unrest?

Due to Sabrina's growing powers and her rebellious attitude, the Magic Council is starting to keep a close eye on her. That could endanger the budding Four Blades movement, especially since one of Sabrina's aunts and guardians, **HILDA**, is a member of the Council herself!

Sabrina's ex-boyfriend, her childhood sweetheart from the Mortal Realm, **HARVEY**, has decided to swear off dating for now in order to focus on school and basketball. But that doesn't mean that he or Sabrina have forgotten how much they mean to each other . . . does it?

Salem here!

You may think I'm just a cat with the gift of gab—but that's just scratching the surface! I'm also an expert on all things magical! After all, I used to be a full-fledged sorcerer, and that's nothing to be taken lightly!

Now, you may think that a magical world is a place where you can use your powers for whatever you want, as much as you want! Well, believe it or not, the Magic Realm has laws, too. Trust me, I found out the hard way!

The Magic Realm is governed by the Council, a group of 7 women, each in charge of a different part of the Realm.

Let me introduce you...

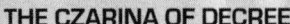

THE CZARINA OF DECREE

That would be Galiena. I just can't stand that frosty witch!
After all, she was the one who personally banished me into
a cat form! But I'm not the only one who dislikes her.
She upholds the laws of the land and deals out punishment.
Some of her favorite punishiments are stripping magic
users of their skills, performing memory wipes, or banishing
magicians into animal forms. As you can plainly see!

THE CZARINA OF CHARITY

Now, Bernadette is a real saint compared to Galiena!
Bernie, as people like to call her, has the job of making
sure that those less fortunate in the Magic Realm
receive assistance. She's always helping to build new
shelters for those whose homes have been destroyed
in magical typhoons or trampled by dragons! And if
anyone is down on their luck and finds it hard to put
bread on the table, Bernie will be there to help!

THE CZARINA OF KNOWLEDGE

Libra maintains the Council library and is an expert on
history. She's also in charge of the education of the
students in the Magic Realm. As a matter of fact,
she's the Headmistress at Sabrina's Charm School,
but she's so shy she tends to stay locked away in her
office all the time!

THE CZARINA OF DEFENSE

Ignacia—who happens to be Libra's older sister—is
probably the only one who scares me as much as
Galiena. She's in charge of the Council armies and
rumor has it that she's very skilled in the art of
magical warfare and helped turn the tide in the
historic Four Blades battle. Luckily, besides that
incident, the Magic Realm has been a pretty peaceful
place overall.

THE CZARINA OF TREASURY

Shimra is a quiet lady who likes to stay out of the spotlight. I can't say I know much more about her except that she's in charge of the Magic Realm economy and taxes, as well as the banking system. She also makes sure that the Council treasury is kept safe. In fact, she's the only one besides the Queen who knows where the riches of the Magic Realm are hidden!

THE CZARINA OF MEDIATION

This is the very spot that Hilda filled after the previous Czarina, Medina, retired. The Czarina of Mediation deals with issues that transcend the Magic Realm into the Mortal realm. That means Hilda's in charge of maintaining magical secrecy in the Magic Realm, and continuing to ensure that mortals do not accidentally witness or experience magic firsthand. Now if she could just keep as good an eye on Sabrina! Sometimes I feel like I'm the babysitter here!

THE CZARINA OF BALANCE, THE QUEEN

Ah, Queen Seles. She's the 7th member of council, and the overseer of all the other departments. She generally allows each Czarina to do her work, but has the power to override any actions or decisions. Lately, some feel that even though she holds the position of leadership, she doesn't actually do as much work as the Czarinas beneath her. No one would say it to her face, though! In fact, she seems kind of scary! I'm just glad I never had to meet her in person!

The council meets every day to go over what needs to be done across the Magic Realm. Every now and then, they have to get together to make an important decision about something—and their personalities sometimes clash! But the point of the Magic Council is cooperation, and most of these ladies have been doing it for hundreds, if not thousands, of years!

Chapter 1

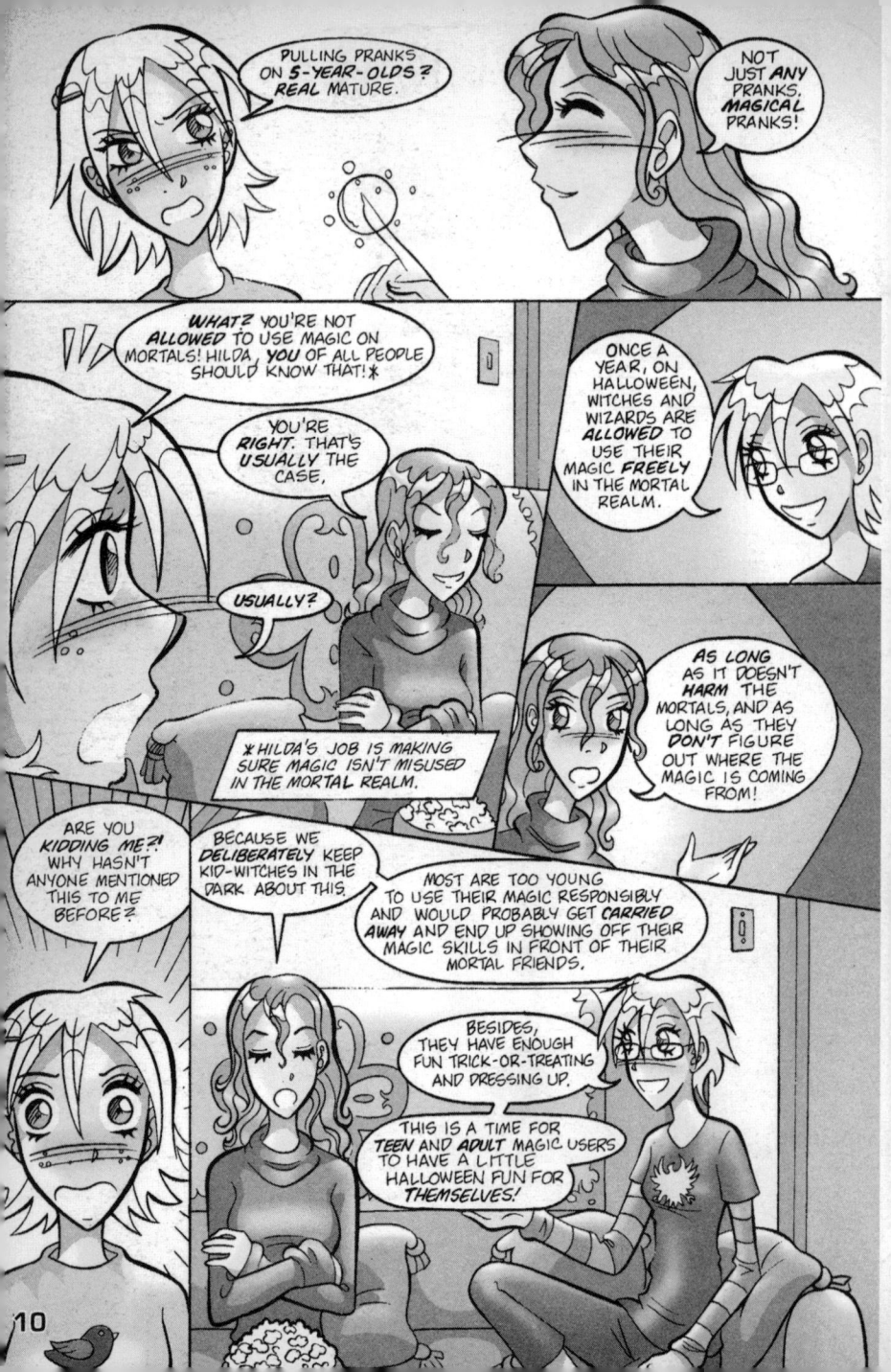

16

THERE'S A BIG FANCY **DOOR** AHEAD.

GUYS...

GO **THROUGH** IT!

THE **CHANDELIER** IS SWINGING...

AND THE **PORTRAITS** IN THE HALL KEEP **LOOKING** AT US AS WE WALK BY!

WITCH

HEH HEH

ZAP

WOOOO

AHHH! IT'S COMING AFTER US!

NICE TRY, SHINJI!

THUNK

HEY!

WITCH

THAT'S THE **8TH** TRICK YOU'VE PLAYED ON US SO FAR, SHINJI!

AS IF THIS HOUSE WASN'T **SCARY** ENOUGH AS IT IS!

HA HA!

ZAP

ZAP

YOW!

27

WE WERE **ROOMMATES** BACK IN CHARM SCHOOL, **WAAAY** BACK.

AW, MAN! WE USED TO PLAY SOME **WICKED** TRICKS ON THE OTHER STUDENTS AND TEACHERS.

SO HOW **DID** YOU GET **EXILED**, ANYWAY?

HEY, DID I **INTRODUCE** YOU TO MY PETS, **LOLA** AND **DAISY**?

UH, HI?

RUFF

YOU **KNOW** IT! WE WERE THE **OFFICIAL** SCHOOL **PRANKSTERS**!

HE DOESN'T WANT TO **SAY** HOW HE GOT **EXILED**... INTERESTING.

WHY IS HE **LOOKING** AT ME THAT WAY? WAS IT SOMETHING I SAID?

HEY, LET'S GET OUT OF THIS **STUFFY** GALLERY AND GO DOWNSTAIRS FOR SOME **PUNCH** AND **PUMPKIN** PIE!

SWEET!

WOW... I DIDN'T **REALIZE** HOW MANY PIECES OF ART IN HERE HAVE TO DO WITH **FOUR BLADES DAY**!

GASP!

28

Chapter 2

HIDDEN POWERS

WRITER & ARTIST:
TANIA DEL RIO

INKS: JIM AMASH
COLORS: JASON JENSEN
LETTERS: TERESA DAVIDSON

ASSISTANT EDITOR:
MIKE PELLERITO

EDITOR:
VICTOR GORELICK

EDITOR-IN-CHIEF:
RICHARD GOLDWATER

AUTUMN'S HERE AGAIN AND I THINK IT'S MAKING ME DEPRESSED...

I KNOW WHAT YOU MEAN. SHORTER DAYS, COLDER NIGHTS... EVERYTHING'S WITHERING AWAY.

AT LEAST IT'S ALWAYS SUNNY IN THE MAGIC REALM BEACH LANDS. SO WHEN I VISIT NARAYAN, IT WILL ALWAYS FEEL LIKE SUMMER!

I KNOW, AND I FEEL REALLY BAD FOR DRAGGING YOU THERE ALL THE TIME TO CAST THAT SPELL ON ME.

I WISH I COULD LEARN TO DO IT MYSELF-- I'VE TRIED BUT IT'S A HARD SPELL TO MASTER...

YEAH, BUT I HAVE TO KEEP CASTING WATER BREATHING SPELLS ON YOU SO YOU CAN VISIT HIM. HE IS A MER-MAN, AFTER ALL!

WELL, I'M WORKING ON A TOP-SECRET SPELL WHICH I THINK MIGHT HELP YOU!

REALLY? TELL ME!

I'M FIGURING OUT A WAY TO COMBINE A COUPLE OTHER SPELLS TO MAKE ONE THAT WILL GIVE NARAYAN LEGS EVERY TIME HE COMES IN CONTACT WITH AIR!

31

WHAT? I'M TELLING THE **TRUTH!** I'M WORKING **REALLY** HARD ON IT!

Uh, THAT'S **GREAT** SABRINA, BUT...

IT'S COMPLETELY **IMPOSSIBLE!** YOU **CAN'T** JUST **INVENT** NEW SPELLS ANY MORE THAN YOU CAN INVENT NEW COLORS.

THERE ARE **NO** NEW SPELLS! ALL THE WITCHES AND WIZARDS FROM THE LAST THOUSANDS OF YEARS HAVE **ALREADY** DISCOVERED AND DOCUMENTED **EVERY** SPELL THAT EXISTS!

WELL, THEY **MIGHT** HAVE MISSED ONE. I'M STILL GONNA TRY!

SABRINA, YOU'RE SO **FUNNY!** YOU ALWAYS KNOW HOW TO MAKE ME SMILE.

I'M **NOT** JOKING, LLANDRA! I'M **SERIOUS** ABOUT THIS! LOOK, LET'S MEET AT THE MAGIC REALM BEACH AFTER CLASS TODAY. I'LL SHOW YOU!

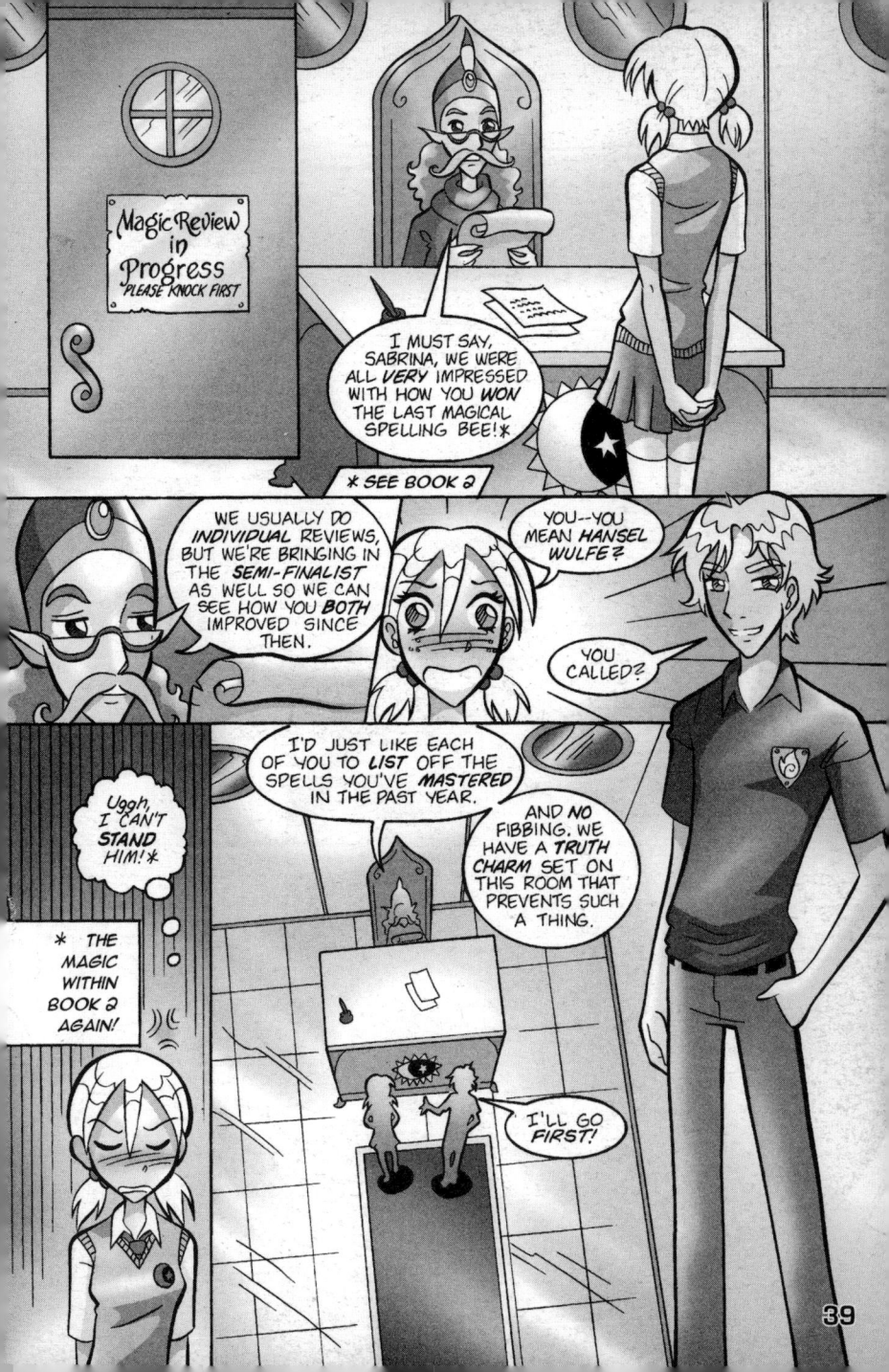

43

Chapter 3

Mortal Decision

WRITER & ARTIST: TANIA DEL RIO · INKS: JIM AMASH
COLORS: JASON JENSEN · LETTERS: TERESA DAVIDSON
ASSISTANT EDITOR: MIKE PELLERITO · EDITOR: VICTOR GORELICK
EDITOR-IN-CHIEF: RICHARD GOLDWATER

Sabrina's Room

SABRINA? SWEETIE? YOU'RE GOING TO BE *LATE* FOR CHARM SCHOOL...

I'M *NOT* GOING!

SHE'S *SERIOUS* ABOUT THIS, ISN'T SHE?

PLEASE, THIS WON'T LAST MORE THAN A WEEK. SABRINA WON'T BE ABLE TO CUT MAGIC OUT OF HER LIFE *THAT* EASILY!

YOU'RE RIGHT, SHE JUST NEEDS A LITTLE TIME. IT WON'T HURT FOR HER TO MISS CHARM SCHOOL ONCE OR TWICE. SHE'S BEEN GOING THROUGH A *ROUGH* TIME...

IT SEEMS THAT WAY. EVER SINCE SHE WAS IMPRISONED BY THE MAGIC COUNCIL FOR HAVING UNUSUAL MAGICAL POWERS, SHE REALLY *HAS* TURNED HER BACK ON MAGIC.

* LAST CHAPTER

SORRY HILDA AND ZELDA, I KNOW YOU THINK I'M JUST BEING *STUBBORN*, BUT I'M NOT GOING TO BE A WITCH ANY MORE! I'M A *MORTAL* -- NOW AND FOREVER!

53

WE KEEP *TRYING* TO TELL HER THAT HER MAGIC SKILLS SHOULD BE *NURTURED*, NOT *REPRESSED!* IT'S A *GIFT*, BUT SHE LOOKS AT IT LIKE A *CURSE*...

KNOCK, KNOCK! ANY *CUTE* WITCHES HOME?

SHINJI! WHAT ARE *YOU* DOING HERE?

DON'T WORRY, HILDA! IT WON'T LAST LONG!

WELL, YOU HAVEN'T BEEN AT CHARM SCHOOL RECENTLY, AND I *MISS* YOU!

PSSH, YOU'RE JUST HERE TO *CONVINCE* ME TO USE MAGIC AGAIN.

WELL, *FORGET* IT! I'M A MORTAL NOW, AND THAT'S *THAT.* NO ONE BELIEVES ME, BUT I AM *TOTALLY* SERIOUS! I WANT TO BE A NORMAL TEENAGE GIRL FOR ONCE!

WELLLL.... THAT TOO...

55

STOMP STOMP

SOMETHING TELLS ME IT DIDN'T GO WELL...

THE NEXT DAY...

WELL, I'M NOT GONNA MOPE AROUND. TODAY'S MY FIRST DAY OF MORTAL HIGH SCHOOL-- AS A **MORTAL!**

YEAH!

LAST NIGHT FEELS LIKE A BAD DREAM. I CAN'T BELIEVE I BROKE UP WITH SHINJI!

SPRO'NG

59

SURE, I DO! I'LL JUST *ZAP* SOME TOAST REAL QUICK!

I MEAN, NO I *WON'T*...

GLOOM

HA HA! I GIVE IT A *DAY*, SABRINA. YOU'LL BE *BACK*. THEY *ALWAYS* COME BACK!

=UGH= SO *COLD* TODAY. BUT I CAN'T USE MAGIC TO *WARM* MY HANDS AND I *DEFINITELY* CAN'T TELEPORT TO SCHOOL.

I'M JUST GONNA HAVE TO DO THIS THE *HARD* WAY!

THIS... ISN'T FUN. AND I'M *ALREADY* RUNNING LATE AS IT IS!

IF I *HURRY* I MIGHT BE ABLE TO GRAB MY BOOKS AND GET TO CLASS BEFORE THE TEACHER GETS TO MY NAME IN *ROLL CALL*!

CLACK CLACK CLACK

63

YOU WERE *RIGHT*, MADDY. THIS PLACE *IS* REALLY COOL!

I KNOW, RIGHT?

WHAT ARE YOU *STARING* AT, SABRINA? YOU THINK HE'S *CUTE*, OR SOMETHING?

WHAT? NO! I WAS JUST THINKING THAT THIS *SMOOTHIE* TASTES ESPECIALLY GOOD BECAUSE HE TOOK THE *TIME* AND *EFFORT* TO MAKE IT FOR ME-- FROM *SCRATCH!*

HE TOOK ALL THE FRUIT AND YOGURT AND BLENDED IT AND... IT JUST SEEMS LIKE *SO* MUCH WORK!

MARK

MAYBE!

Uhhh, *RIGHT.* AND WHAT *ELSE* WAS HE GONNA DO? MAKE IT APPEAR OUT OF *THIN* AIR?

HA HA, YOU'RE SO WEIRD!

LLANDRA! WHAT ARE YOU DOING HERE?

WE HAD **PLANS** TO HANG OUT TONIGHT, BUT YOU OBVIOUSLY FORGOT!

AND WHO MIGHT **THIS** BE?

THIS IS MY FRIEND, **MADELINE**. SHE'S A MOR--er, I MEAN...

I SEE...

SO YOU'RE REALLY **OUT** WITH THE OLD AND IN WITH THE **NEW**, huh? YOU'LL JUST **TOSS** OUT YOUR OLD FRIENDS WITH THE REST OF THE BATH WATER, IS THAT IT?

IT--IT'S NOT LIKE THAT...

WHAT IS SHE TALKING ABOUT? WHAT **HAPPENED**?

A **MORTAL** LIKE **YOU** WOULDN'T UNDERSTAND!

MORTAL? WHO ARE YOU CALLING A MORTAL AND WHAT DOES THAT MAKE **YOU**?

MADDY, DON'T LISTEN TO HER. SHE'S **CRAZY**.

THINGS NEVER WORKED BETWEEN US BEFORE BECAUSE I WAS ALWAYS **HIDING** PART OF MYSELF FROM HIM, BUT NOW THAT I'M A MORTAL, THERE'S **NOTHING** LEFT TO HIDE.

WE CAN BE TWO **NORMAL** TEENAGERS, HAPPY TOGETHER!

BONK

ACK!

SORRY ABOUT THAT! IT **RICOCHETED** OFF THE HOOP!

ALRIGHT, LET'S TAKE FIVE!

SABRINA? WHAT IS **SHE** DOING HERE? SHE HASN'T SPOKEN TO ME SINCE I TOLD AMY I WANTED NOTHING TO DO WITH EITHER OF THEM...*

* SEE BOOK 2

69

Chapter 4

S-SALEM?! IS THAT YOU?!

Salem Returns

I THINK THIS HAS GONE *TOO FAR.*

AGREED!

WRITER & ARTIST: TANIA DEL RIO
INKS: JIM AMASH · COLORS: JASON JENSEN
LETTERS: TERESA DAVIDSON
ASSISTANT EDITOR: MIKE PELLERITO · EDITOR: VICTOR GORELICK
EDITOR-IN-CHIEF: RICHARD GOLDWATER

SABRINA HASN'T USED MAGIC IN OVER A *MONTH* NOW, AND SHE'S REALLY SET ON BECOMING A MORTAL. BUT *"WIZARDS' WEEKLY"* STATES THAT *IGNORING* YOUR MAGICAL SKILLS CAN BE *DETRIMENTAL* TO YOUR HEALTH!

BUT SHE CAN BE SO *STUBBORN!* WE'VE ALREADY TRIED *PLEADING, BEGGING* AND *CAJOLING.* IT ONLY SEEMS TO MAKE HER *MORE* DETERMINED TO BE A MORTAL. WHAT *ELSE* IS THERE THAT WE CAN DO?

MAYBE IT'S TIME TO TRY A *DIFFERENT* TACTIC...

WHAT DO YOU MEAN?

WIZARDS

SPELLS AND YOUR HEALTH

JUST LEAVE IT TO ME! FEW TEENAGE GIRLS CAN RESIST THE APPEAL OF *CUDDLY KITTEN* EYES! BESIDES, WE'RE ALREADY FORGETTING A BIG PART OF WHAT MAKES SABRINA TICK: HER *EGO!*

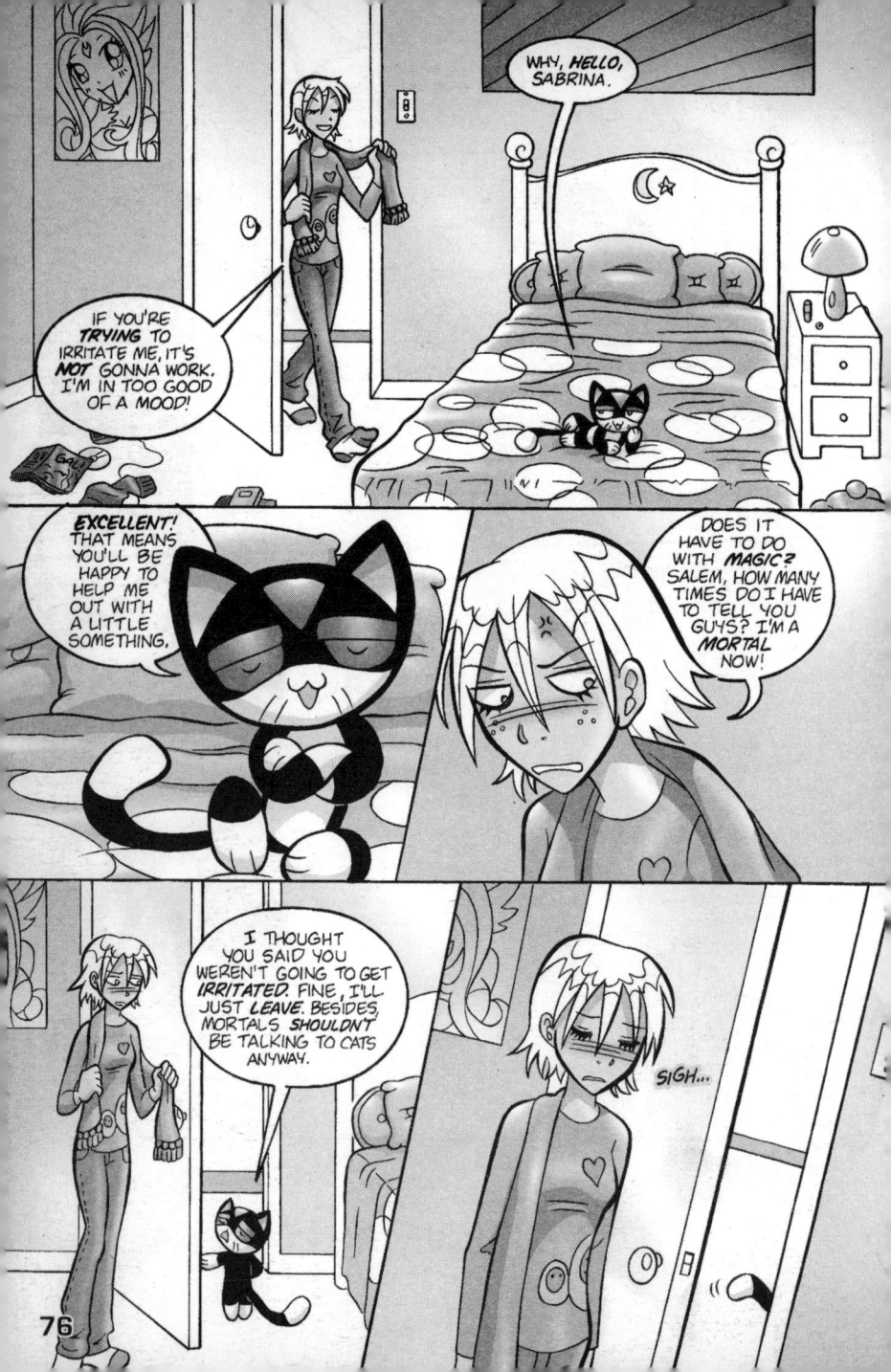

WAIT, SALEM. TELL ME WHAT YOU WANT.

IT'S JUST THAT, I'VE BEEN *STUCK* IN THIS KITTY CAT BODY FOR 1,010 LONG YEARS NOW... YOU KEEP SAYING YOU WISH YOU WERE A NORMAL TEENAGE GIRL, BUT WHAT ABOUT *ME?*

SOMETIMES I WISH I COULD BE A *NORMAL* HUMAN WIZARD LIKE I *USED* TO BE!

heh

POUNCE

I'M *SORRY* ABOUT THAT, SALEM, REALLY, BUT THERE'S NOTHING I CAN DO ABOUT THAT. IT'S YOUR *ETERNAL PUNISHMENT* FOR TRYING TO TAKE OVER THE WORLD!

BUT HASN'T THIS *PUNISHMENT* GONE ON LONG ENOUGH? I DON'T WANT THE WORLD ANYMORE-- I JUST WANT *OPPOSABLE THUMBS!*

ANYWAY, ALTHOUGH YOU *MAY* HAVE THE POWER TO GIVE A MER-MAN LEGS AND TO BRING DEAD PLANTS BACK TO LIFE, TURNING A CAT INTO A MAN IS *COMPLETELY* BEYOND YOUR SKILL. IT'S *SILLY* TO EVEN THINK YOU COULD.

WAIT A MINUTE. I MEAN, THEY *DO* SAY I'VE GOT SOME SPECIAL MAGICAL ABILITIES. I BET I *COULD* DO IT IF I REALLY WANTED TO. BUT IT WOULDN'T BE *RIGHT!*

AND, BESIDES, YOU'RE A *MORTAL* NOW, ANYWAY. MORTALS CAN'T DO ANYTHING AS *IMPRESSIVE* AS THAT.

"RIGHT.

LATER...

hmm

SABRINA! ARE YOU ACTUALLY *READING* THROUGH SOME *SPELL* BOOKS?!

DON'T GET TOO EXCITED. IT'S JUST A *ONE-TIME* THING!

WELL! SALEM MUST HAVE SAID THE *RIGHT* THING. I WONDER WHAT SHE'S RESEARCHING?

I HOPE IT'S NOTHING *BAD*...

85

SLURP

RUSTLE

CRUNCH CRUNCH

...

YES, SALEM?

FOOD! WHERE'S MY BREAKFAST?

YOU'RE A GROWN MAN, SALEM. GET YOUR OWN BREAKFAST. UNLESS YOU WANT TO EAT DRY KIBBLE AGAIN.

HUMAN CEREAL IS A LOT LIKE KIBBLE, HUH? I BET IT TASTES BETTER THOUGH! I'LL TRY THAT!

WHAT?! NO!

MILK

SPLASH

87

POUNCE

DARN! I *MISSED!*

I CAN HARDLY BELIEVE YOU WERE EVER A *THREAT* TO THE MAGIC REALM.

IT WAS 1,010 YEARS AGO. GIMME A BREAK!

SALEM, YOU *REALLY* HAVE TO MAKE AN EFFORT NOT TO GIVE IN TO YOUR FELINE *INSTINCTS.* YOU'RE MAKING PEOPLE *NERVOUS!*

SORRY. SORRY.

SOON...

BAT BAT.

91

Chapter 5

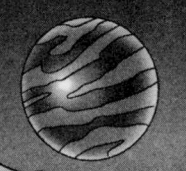

GRUNT URRRRGH

URRGH! THIS PLACE REALLY *IS* RECLUSIVE! AND IT'S RIGHT IN THE MIDDLE OF THE MAGIC FOREST SO I CAN'T EVEN FLY HERE ON MY BROOM.*

WAIT A MINUTE... IF IT'S NEARLY IMPOSSIBLE TO USE MAGIC IN A MAGICAL FOREST, WHY AM I COMING HERE FOR TRAINING?

*WITCHES' MAGICAL ABILITIES ARE SUPPRESSED WITHIN A MAGIC FOREST. --EDITOR

WAAGH!

FLAP

CRUMBLE

FLAP

ONE HOUR LATER...

UUGGH... FINALLY!

WHAP

OOOHH... FEEL.... *NAUSEOUS*...

TWO HOURS LATER...

HUH? WHERE AM I?

WHAT THE *HECK!* I PASS OUT FROM MAGICAL *EXERTION,* AND YOU JUST LEAVE ME ON THE FLOOR LIKE THIS?!

OH.

HMM?OH, WELCOME BACK!

I DIDN'T *GO* ANYWHERE YOU OLD--

YOU *PASSED,* BY THE WAY.

"...SUCH AS CLIMBING BACK DOWN THE CLIFF ON YOUR WAY HOME... DISMISSED!"

URGGH! BATTY OLD BARTHOLOMEW! WHO DOES HE THINK HE IS?!

HOW'D YOUR FIRST DAY OF TUTORING GO?

DON'T... EVEN... ASK.

STOMP STOMP

WELL, SHE'S CRANKY, SO THAT MEANS SHE MUST HAVE BEEN WORKING HARD!

I BET SHE'S LEARNING A LOT!

SO...TIRED... AND I STILL HAVE TO GO TO MORTAL SCHOOL TOMORROW MORNING.

FLOP!

THE NEXT DAY...

113

Chapter 6

HOW WAS IT TODAY?

WONDERFUL. THAT IS, IF YOU CONSIDER *CLAWING* YOUR WAY OUT OF A *20-FOOT* WELL A GOOD TIME. THIS TUTOR IS A *HACK!*

DRIP DRIP

MAYBE YOU JUST DON'T *UNDERSTAND* HIS METHODS. HE WAS ONCE ONE OF THE *GREATEST* WIZARDS IN THE MAGIC REALM.

NOT *ANYMORE!* I'M NOT EVEN CONVINCED HE CAN *USE* MAGIC AT ALL! I WANT TO GO BACK TO *CHARM SCHOOL!*

GIVE IT A BIT MORE TIME, SABRINA. YOU NEED A PLACE WHERE YOU CAN FREELY EXPLORE YOUR MAGICAL *POTENTIAL.*

CHARM SCHOOL IS RUN BY *CZARINA LIBRA* OF THE MAGIC COUNCIL. IT'S JUST *TOO* EASY FOR THEM TO KEEP AN EYE ON YOU AND YOUR UNIQUE ABILITIES THERE.

118

IT'S FROM *LLANDRA!* SHE HASN'T SPOKEN TO ME SINCE I TRIED TO *QUIT* MAGIC! *

SHE DROPPED BY EARLIER TONIGHT. I THINK SHE MISSES YOU, 'BRINA.

* SEE CHAPTER 3

WHAT'S IT SAY?

WELL?

MAYBE IT'S AN *APOLOGY!*

PSSH.

IT'S AN INVITATION TO *NARAYAN'S* BIRTHDAY PARTY TOMORROW NIGHT. WHO'S *THAT?*

FLOP

IT'S LLANDRA'S *MERMAN* BOYFRIEND.

I GAVE HIM THE ABILITY TO WALK ON LAND AND THAT'S *PARTIALLY* WHAT GOT ME IN TROUBLE WITH THE MAGIC COUNCIL.*

LLANDRA'S BEEN SPENDING *ALL* HER TIME WITH HIM EVER SINCE.

SHE WOULDN'T HAVE SENT THIS TO YOU IF SHE DIDN'T WANT TO BE YOUR *FRIEND.* YOU SHOULD GO! AND BRING ME TOO, SO I CAN EAT SOME *CAKE!*

I DUNNO... *SHINJI'S* GONNA BE THERE FOR SURE. IT'S BAD ENOUGH *AVOIDING* HIM AT SCHOOL.

* CHAPTER 2

120

123

125

127

131

SWOOP

eek!

WOAH! HEEEY!

DRAG

OW! OW!

OOOWW!

GRRR

AND THEN THE FAIRY SAID "LEARN IT YOURSELF!"

PLEASE, STOP! I JUST WANT TO KNOW HOW YOU CAN USE MAGIC IN A MAGIC FOREST!

HO HO HO! GOOD ADVICE THERE.

SCRATCH

CHOMP

CAN YOU TEACH ME?

132

Chapter 7

Truth be Told

WRITER & ARTIST~ **TANIA DEL RIO** · INKER~ *JIM AMASH*
COLORS ~ **JASON JENSEN** · *LETTERS* ~ **TERESA DAVIDSON**
ASSISTANT EDITOR~ **MIKE PELLERITO** · *EDITOR* ~ **VICTOR GORELICK**
EDITOR-IN-CHIEF~ **RICHARD GOLDWATER**

=GASP=!

WELL, WELL, WHAT HAVE WE *HERE?*

139

SO WE'RE HEADED TO THE *SECRET* MEETING SITE OF THE *FOUR BLADES?*

YEP! SHINJI WILL BE *SO* HAPPY TO HEAR THAT YOU WANT TO *REJOIN* THE EFFORT, SABRINA! AND THE STUFF YOU BROUGHT FROM YOUR TUTOR WILL REALLY HELP US OUT!

ALTHOUGH... I'M REALLY SORRY TO SAY THAT WE *CAN'T* RETURN YOU TO YOUR ORIGINAL LEADERSHIP POSITION AS ONE OF THE FOUR BLADES. BUT THERE'S *ALWAYS* ROOM FOR MORE *RENEGADE BLADES* TO HELP OUT THE CAUSE!

SO I TAKE IT THAT SHINJI'S NEW *GIRLFRIEND* IS STILL AROUND?

HEMLOCK? YEAH. I ADMIT I WASN'T SURE WHAT TO MAKE OF HER AT FIRST. IT SEEMED LIKE SHE CAME OUT OF NOWHERE, BUT SHE'S REALLY PUT *EVERYTHING* INTO THE FOUR BLADES-- SHE'S PROVEN HERSELF TO BE A REALLY ORGANIZED AND DEDICATED *LEADER!*

Hmph.

I DON'T CARE WHAT LLANDRA AND SHINJI THINK. I *DON'T* TRUST THIS GIRL AND I THINK THEY'RE GIVING HER *TOO MUCH* POWER. I'M GONNA KEEP MY EYE ON HER, *THAT'S* FOR SURE!

Hmph, IT DOESN'T MEAN *ANYTHING*. YOU *COULD* SAY THEY WERE TRYING TO HELP THE QUEEN BY REMOVING HER FROM THE THRONE, IT WAS FOR HER *OWN* GOOD, AFTER ALL!

BUT THAT *DOESN'T* MAKE ANY SENSE! I MEAN--

SABRINA, THE POINT IS, IT'S AN *OLD* DOCUMENT AND IT DOESN'T *MATTER* WHAT IT SAYS OR WHAT IT MEANS. WHAT MATTERS IS *NOW*. AND WE HAVE A SPECIAL *MISSION* FOR YOU.

YOU DO?

THAT'S RIGHT. IF WE'RE GOING TO *CONVINCE* THE REST OF THE REALM THAT THE MANA TREE REALLY *IS* DYING, WE'RE GOING TO NEED SOLID *PROOF!* WE NEED *YOU* TO GO TO THE MANA TREE AND BRING BACK SOME OF ITS DYING *LEAVES!*

WHAT? THAT'S *IMPOSSIBLE!* THE MANA TREE IS ON THE FLOATING ISLAND OF *SYLPHANAR!!* ONLY THE QUEEN HERSELF CAN GO THERE!

BUT LLANDRA WAS THERE *TOO!* WHY NOT HER?

BUT YOU WERE THERE ONCE BEFORE! AND YOU WERE PERMITTED BY THE SPIRIT OF *SYLPHANAR!* HIMSELF TO GET *CLOSE* TO THE MANA TREE. *

SABRINA, WE ALL KNOW YOU HAVE *SPECIAL* MAGICAL ABILITIES THAT NO ONE ELSE DOES! IF ANYONE CAN FIGURE OUT HOW TO GET BACK THERE -- *YOU CAN!*

* BOOK 2

I--I'LL TRY MY BEST...

145

151

Chapter 8

LET'S FACE IT. HE CAN *BARELY* ACKNOWLEDGE OUR RELATIONSHIP IN FRONT OF HIS FRIENDS. HOW COULD I EXPECT HIM TO INTRODUCE ME TO HIS FAMILY?

I TOLD HIM MY MAGICAL SECRET--I'VE TOLD HIM EVERYTHING ABOUT ME, AND HE STILL ISN'T READY TO BE OPEN WITH OUR RELATIONSHIP!

IT ISN'T FAIR...

LATER...

HOW ARE THINGS PROGRESSING WITH EVERYONE?

GOOD, SO FAR! WE NOW HAVE 45 MEMBERS, WITH MORE JOINING EVERY WEEK!

HOW CAN YOU *TRUST* ALL THESE PEOPLE? HOW DO YOU KNOW THAT ONE OF THEM WON'T TELL THE MAGIC COUNCIL...

...THAT WE'RE *PLOTTING* AGAINST THE QUEEN?

THAT'S JUST A *RISK* WE HAVE TO TAKE.

THE ONLY GOOD THING IS THAT ALL OUR MEMBERS ARE *KIDS* OUR AGE. EVEN IF ONE OF THEM TRIED TO TELL THE MAGIC COUNCIL, CHANCES ARE THEY *WOULDN'T* BE TAKEN SERIOUSLY!

ADULTS DON'T GIVE US ENOUGH *CREDIT!*

162

173

MAN, I'M NOT *USED* TO GOING TO BED *THIS EARLY!* I'M A WITCH! I'M PRACTICALLY *NOCTURNAL!*

SHINJI AND LLANDRA ARE IN CHARM SCHOOL RIGHT NOW. I MISS CHARM SCHOOL. I MISS SEEING ALL MY FRIENDS THERE...

SKITCH SKITCH

WHAT'S *THAT?!*

COCKA DOODLE DOO!

174

175

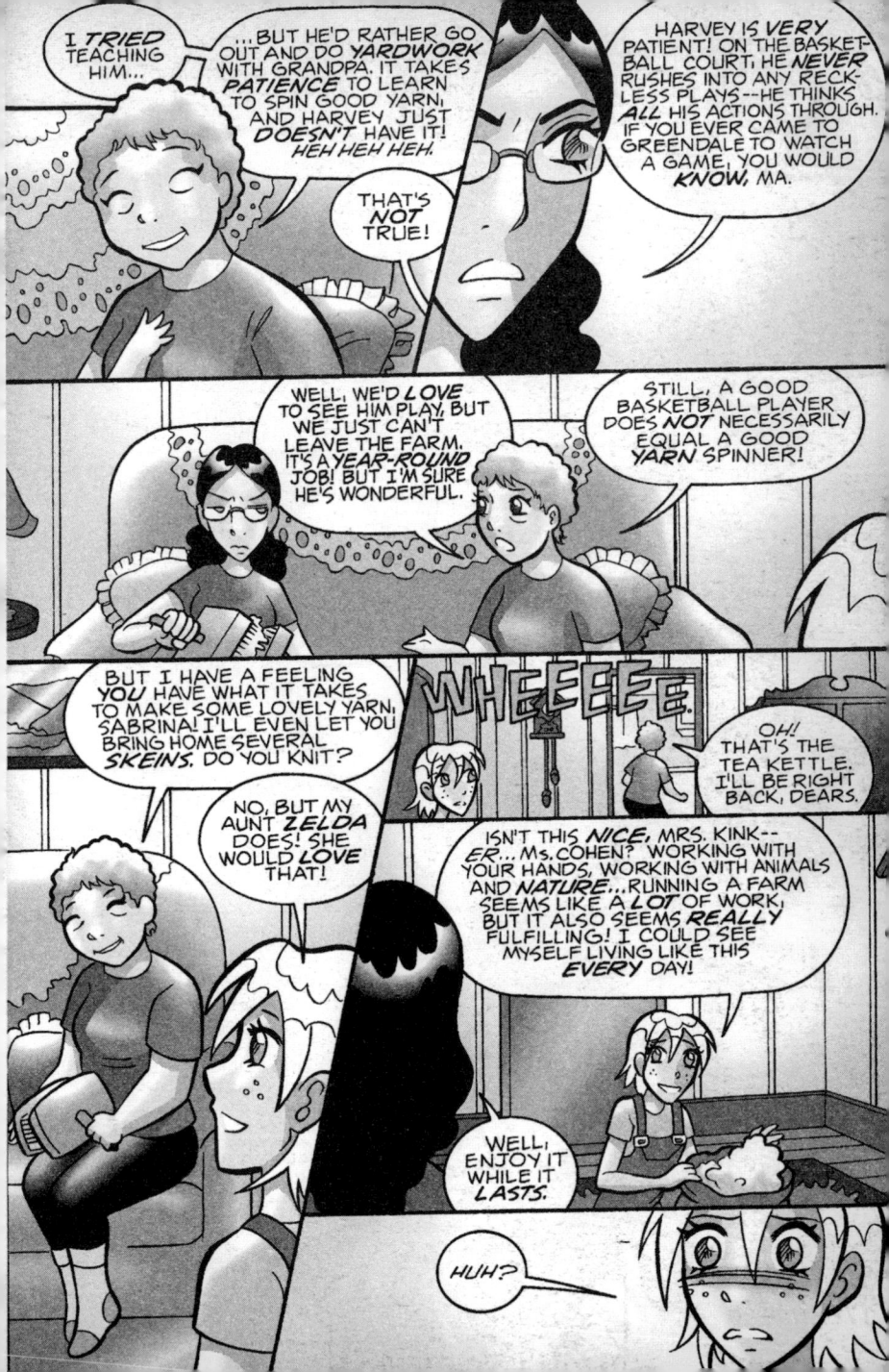

Panel 1:

I'M *NOT* JUST TALKING ABOUT THE *FARM*. I'M ALSO TALKING ABOUT YOUR LITTLE *RELATIONSHIP* WITH MY HARVEY. SUMMER FUN IS *FINE*, BUT SCHOOL IS STARTING AGAIN SOON...AND HARVEY NEEDS TO *FOCUS*.

WHAT ARE YOU *SAYING?*

I'M SAYING...

Panel 2:

...THAT I WILL *NOT* ALLOW HARVEY TO BE IN ANY RELATIONSHIPS UNTIL HE GETS INTO A *GOOD COLLEGE*. HE'S TOO *YOUNG* TO BE WRAPPED UP WITH GIRLS, AND HE HAS *TOO* MUCH TALENT TO WASTE IT ALL ON DAYDREAMING AND *ROMANCE*.

YOU *SAY* THAT NOW, BUT WHAT HAPPENS IF HARVEY GETS ACCEPTED INTO A *DIFFERENT* SCHOOL THAN *YOU?* HE MAY CHANGE HIS MIND ABOUT GOING SO HE CAN BE WITH YOU! BELIEVE ME, I SPEAK FROM *EXPERIENCE!*

Ms. COHEN! I WANT HARVEY TO SUCCEED AT BASKETBALL JUST AS MUCH AS *YOU* DO! I'M NOT TRYING TO STAND IN HIS WAY--I *SUPPORT* HIM ALL THE WAY!

I WOULDN'T LET THAT HAPPEN! HARVEY *KNOWS* BETTER THAN THAT!

Panel 3:

LOVE DOES *CRAZY* THINGS TO PEOPLE'S JUDGMENT, SABRINA. I INTEND TO *STOP* THIS LITTLE ROMANCE *BEFORE* IT GETS TO THAT POINT. ONCE YOU ARE *ADULTS*, YOU ARE FREE TO DATE ALL YOU WANT. BUT FOR NOW, I THINK IT'S BEST THAT YOU *TONE* IT DOWN.

Panel 4:

I CAN'T *BELIEVE* WHAT I'M HEARING! NO *WONDER* HARVEY IS ALWAYS SO TIMID ABOUT GETTING INTO RELATIONSHIPS....!

HIS MOM IS *TELLING* HIM WHAT TO DO! SHE'S COMPLETELY *CONTROLLING* HIS LIFE! I GOTTA TALK TO HARVEY ABOUT THIS! IT *ISN'T* RIGHT!

A New Leaf

WRITER & ARTIST
TANIA DEL RIO

INKS · **JIM AMASH**

COLORS · **JASON JENSEN**

LETTERS · **TERESA DAVIDSON**

ASSISTANT EDITOR
MIKE PELLERITO

EDITOR · **VICTOR GORELICK**

EDITOR-IN-CHIEF
RICHARD GOLDWATER

AFTER THEY PASS, THE COAST SHOULD BE CLEAR...

I WISH SHINJI AND THE **FOUR BLADES** DIDN'T GIVE ME SUCH A **DIFFICULT** MISSION.

BUT MAYBE OPENING A PORTAL FROM WITHIN A **NATURAL** SETTING IN THE MAGIC REALM WILL WORK BETTER THAN WHEN I TRIED DOING IT FROM MY **BEDROOM!**

HOW AM I SUPPOSED TO GET TO THE **FLOATING ISLAND** OF **SYLPHANARI** ON MY OWN? I'VE **ALREADY** TRIED OPENING PORTALS AND FLYING THERE ON MY BROOM, BUT NEITHER ONE HAS **WORKED!**

VISUALIZE...

VISUALIZE...

183

Chapter 9

I WONDER IF **BARTHOLOMEW** COULD HELP ME THINK OF A WAY TO GET TO THE FLOATING ISLAND. IT'S **RISKY** TO ASK HIM BECAUSE ONLY THE QUEEN IS **TECHNICALLY** PERMITTED TO GO THERE...

BUT I **SHOULD** BE ABLE TO TRUST HIM! HE USED TO BE A MEMBER OF THE **OLD FOUR BLADES** MOVEMENT. ✱

EXCEPT HIS MEMORY'S BEEN **WIPED** AND HE CAN'T REMEMBER ANY OF IT...

✱ SEE CHAPTER 7

Um, BARTHOLOMEW? DO YOU KNOW ABOUT THE FLOATING ISLAND OF **SYLPHANARI**?

DO I ?! WHY, IT'S ONLY THE **MOST** LUXURIOUS VACATION SPOT IN THE **ENTIRE** MAGIC REALM! I USED TO GO THERE QUITE A BIT DURING MY **YOUTH**!

OF COURSE, HE DOESN'T KNOW THAT THE RESORT THERE IS **LONG GONE** AND THAT THE ISLAND IS SLOWLY **DYING**-- ALONG WITH THE **MANA TREE**!

WHAT DO YOU MEAN **IT'S GONE**?

I **FORGOT** YOU CAN READ MY MIND...

YEAH, BUT IT'S NO LONGER--

188

189

WELCOME BACK, YOUNG ONE. DO YOU REMEMBER THE **WORD OF ENTRY?** THERE HAVE BEEN MANY **TRICKSTERS** ATTEMPTING TO BREAK THROUGH MY WALL. BUT ONLY **YOU** WOULD KNOW THE WORD I SEEK.

YES! **SATIREV.** *

* THE MAGIC WITHIN BOOK 2

REMEMBER **ALL** YOU SEE AND KEEP IT CLOSE TO YOUR **HEART.**

TIME GROWS SHORT, YET **DANGER** SIMPLY GROWS.

SOON...

IT DOESN'T **LOOK** LIKE IT'S DYING! MOST OF ITS LEAVES ARE **STILL** GREEN!

SO WHY CAN'T I **FIND** ANY? LAST TIME I WAS HERE, THERE WERE **SEVERAL** LAYING AROUND! YOU WOULD THINK THERE'D BE EVEN **MORE** NOW!

"MOST" OF THEM, YEAH. BUT THE MANA TREE ISN'T EVEN **SUPPOSED** TO HAVE **ONE** BROWN LEAF! IT KEEPS **SHEDDING** THEM, AND THAT'S WHAT I HAVE TO BRING BACK FOR MY MISSION!

WELL, IT'S A **BIG** TREE. LET'S WALK AROUND TO THE OTHER SIDE.

199

Chapter 10

A Night to FORGET

WRITER & ARTIST · TANIA DEL RIO ~ INKS · JIM AMASH ~ COLORS · JASON JENSEN
LETTERS · TERESA DAVIDSON ~ EDITOR · MIKE PELLERITO
MANAGING EDITOR · VICTOR GORELICK ~ EDITOR-IN-CHIEF · RICHARD GOLDWATER

HARVEY...

THIS WAS SUPPOSED TO BE A **HAPPY** NIGHT -- FILLED WITH CANDY AND MAGIC TRICKS.

BUT THIS IS THE **WORST** TRICK OF ALL.

IN FACT, IT'S NOT EVEN A **TRICK** -- IT'S THE WORST NIGHT OF MY **LIFE**...

...AND HARVEY WILL **NEVER** KNOW WHY.

EARLIER...

IF YOU KIDS *REALLY* WANT TO THROW A HALLOWEEN PARTY IN MY "HAUNTED HOUSE", THAT'S FINE BY ME...

...BUT I'LL BE *AWAY* ON OTHER BUSINESS THAT NIGHT. COULD YOU GUYS DO ME A FAVOR AND MAKE SURE NO ONE GOES INTO MY *GALLERY?*

AWESOME! THANKS, RUUNE! AND I WILL *PERSONALLY* GUARD YOUR GALLERY FROM PRYING EYES!

Uh, THAT INCLUDES *YOU* TOO, SHINJI!

HOLD ON! AUNT HILDA WON'T LET ME GO TO THIS PARTY IF THERE ISN'T SOMEONE *SUPERVISING!*

HILDA DOESN'T HAVE TO WORRY. LOLA AND DAISY WILL MAKE SURE EVERYONE *BEHAVES.* HEH HEH HEH.

YEEP.

GRRR

ALRIGHT, GUYS, LET'S SET UP! THIS IS GOING TO BE THE *BEST* HALLOWEEN PARTY EVER!

*RUUNE IS AN EXILE OF THE MAGIC KINGDOM AND AN OLD FRIEND OF SALEM (WHEN HE WAS HUMAN) FROM CHARM SCHOOL.

* SEE BOOK 2

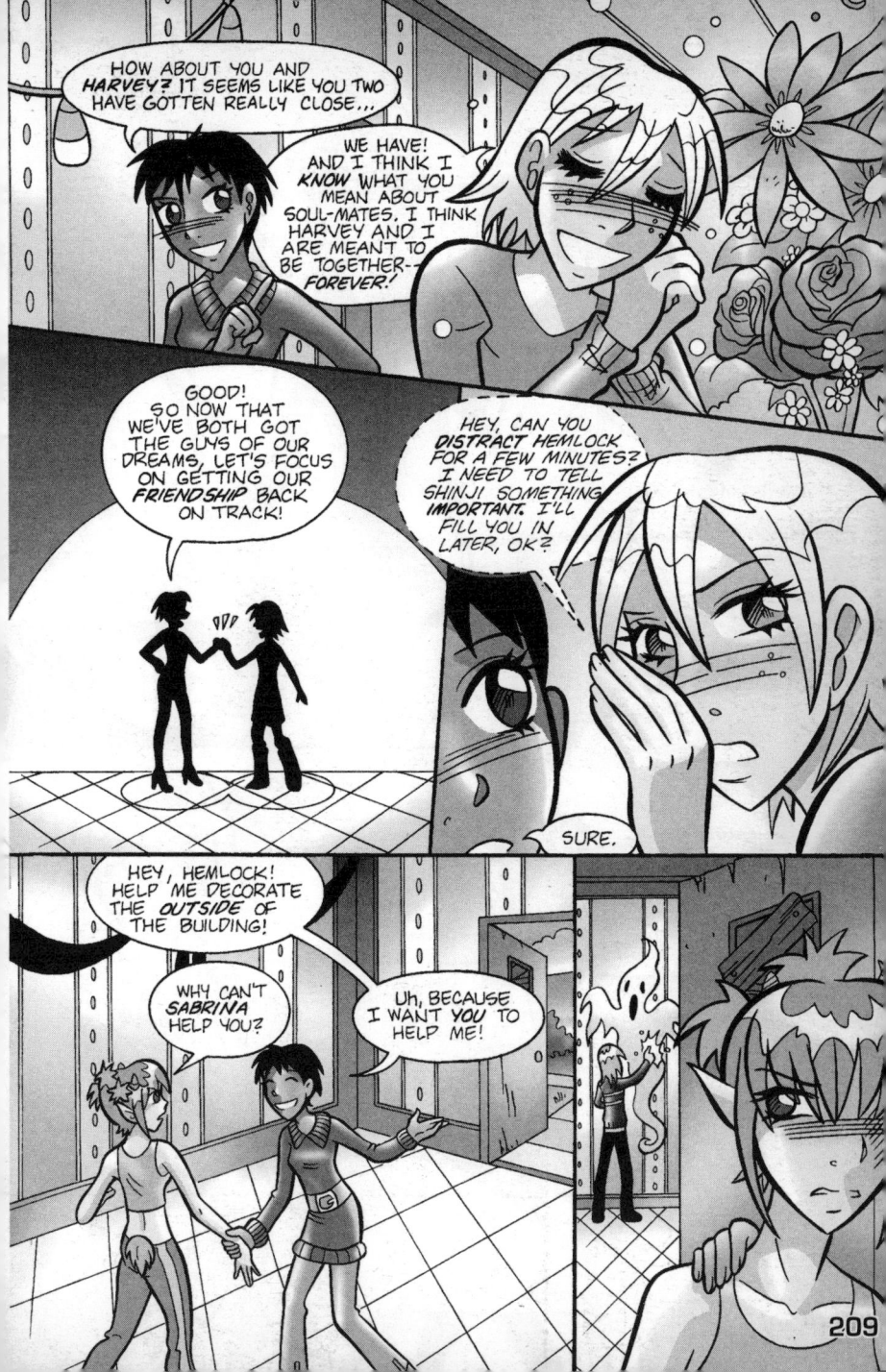

209

211

≥ SIGH≤... LOOK AT THEM. I GUESS IT'S **OFFICIAL**. HARVEY REALLY **DOES** WANT TO BE WITH SABRINA.

I'VE TRIED AND I'VE **TRIED** TO GET HARVEY TO LIKE ME. BUT I GIVE UP.

EVEN A **FOOL** CAN SEE THOSE TWO ARE IN LOVE. I'M **NOT** GOING TO GET BETWEEN THEM ANY MORE.

YOU OK?

YEAH... I THINK SO.

AMY, DON'T WORRY. THERE ARE **PLENTY** MORE FISH IN THE SEA.

219

FREEZE!

AH!

WHO ARE YOU? WHAT ARE YOU DOING IN MY NIECE'S ROOM? *EXPLAIN* YOURSELF OR I WILL PERSONALLY ESCORT YOU TO THE MAGIC COUNCIL FOR *INTERROGATION!*

THINK FAST!

DO YOU SEE WHAT THIS IS? THIS IS A *LEAF* FROM THE *MANA TREE.*

AND DO YOU WANT TO KNOW *WHO'S* BEEN HIDING THIS? *SABRINA!*

WORSE YET, SHE BROUGHT A *MORTAL* WITH HER. THAT'S RIGHT, HER *BOYFRIEND* HARVEY.

SHE BROKE ONTO THE FLOATING ISLAND AND *STOLE* THIS LEAF FROM THE *SACRED* MANA TREE!

A *FILTHY* MORTAL *TOUCHED* THE SACRED MANA TREE THAT ONLY THE *QUEEN* HERSELF CAN VISIT. AND ALL BECAUSE *SABRINA* BROUGHT HIM THERE!

I-IT'S *IMPOSSIBLE!*

IS IT *REALLY?* MAYBE FOR *MOST* OF US, BUT YOU KNOW AS WELL AS I DO THAT SABRINA HAS *UNIQUE* POWERS. SHE CAN DO THINGS *NO ONE* ELSE CAN. SHE CAN GET TO THE FLOATING ISLAND AND SHE CAN BRING MORTALS *WITH* HER.

SHE CAN CAUSE A LEAF FROM THE IMMORTAL MANA TREE TO *DIE.* DO YOU SEE WHAT SHE HAS DONE?

THE *PROOF* IS RIGHT HERE!

WHAT?!

YOU **STILL** HAVEN'T TOLD ME WHO YOU ARE OR WHAT YOU'RE DOING HERE!

I'M AN **HONEST,** QUEEN-LOVING CITIZEN OF THE MAGIC REALM. I BROKE INTO SABRINA'S ROOM TO GET THIS **EVIDENCE** TO SHOW THE MAGIC COUNCIL.

Hmm, I BET THE REST OF THE COUNCIL WOULD BE PRETTY **UPSET** TO HEAR ABOUT THIS.

AFTER ALL, ISN'T IT YOUR **JOB** TO **PREVENT** MORTALS FROM KNOWING ABOUT MAGIC? BUT HERE WE HAVE A MORTAL WHO NOT ONLY KNOWS ABOUT MAGIC, BUT WHO **TOUCHED** THE MOST SACRED TREE IN OUR REALM. AND YOUR **NIECE** IS TO BLAME.

Tut tut. **WHAT** WILL THE COUNCIL THINK?

HOW CAN YOU BE **ANY** GOOD AT YOUR JOB WHEN EVEN YOUR **OWN** FAMILY MEMBER IS ABLE TO COMMIT SUCH TERRIBLE **CRIMES** BENEATH YOUR NOSE?

STOP IT!

KRACKLE

WHAT YOU SAY MAY BE TRUE, BUT YOU ARE A **TRESPASSER** IN MY HOME AND I HAVE A RIGHT TO CAPTURE YOU AND TURN YOU OVER TO THE **AUTHORITIES!**

WAIT! IF YOU LET ME GO, YOU CAN **KEEP** THE EVIDENCE TO DESTROY.

RELEASE ME AND YOU CAN USE THIS CHANCE TO **RIGHT** THE WRONG YOUR NIECE HAS CAUSED AND **SAVE** YOUR CAREER. IN RETURN, I WON'T TELL THE COUNCIL. THEY WOULDN'T BELIEVE ME UNLESS I HAD **PROOF,** ANYWAY.

221

223

≋GASP!≋ WAS HEMLOCK TELLING THE *TRUTH?* DID SABRINA *BETRAY* ME?

PARTY'S OVER! EVERYONE OUT-- NOW!!

SHE *KNOWS* ABOUT THE FOUR BLADES! WE'RE DOOMED! SABRINA, HOW COULD YOU *DO THIS?!*

HILDA! WHAT IS GOING ON?

THAT'S WHAT *I'D* LIKE TO KNOW!

IS IT *TRUE,* SABRINA? DID YOU GO TO THE FLOATING ISLAND? DID YOU BRING *HARVEY* WITH YOU? DID YOU REALLY TAKE A LEAF FROM THE MANA TREE?

W-WHO-- HOW DID--

YES OR *NO,* SABRINA? IS THIS TRUE OR NOT?

225

Chapter 11

SHATTERED LIVES

WRITER AND ARTIST: TANIA DEL RIO

INKS: JIM AMASH COLORS: JASON JENSEN
LETTERS: PHIL FELIX
EDITOR: MIKE PELLERITO
MANAGING EDITOR: VICTOR GORELICK
EDITOR-IN-CHIEF: RICHARD GOLDWATER

WHAT *IS* THIS STUFF?!

I'M HAVING A *YARD SALE!*

WHAT?! BUT WE'RE IN THE MIDDLE OF *NOWHERE!*

229

YOUR MOTHER **ALREADY** KNEW YOUR FATHER WAS A WITCH WHEN SHE MARRIED HIM. THE REASON THEY GOT DIVORCED WAS BECAUSE SHE **DIDN'T** APPROVE OF HIM JOINING THE FOUR BLADES. HE SPENT **MORE** TIME IN THE MAGIC REALM, PLOTTING TO OVERTHROW THE QUEEN THAN HE DID IN THE MORTAL REALM WITH HER-- AND YOU.

THE PROBLEM WAS, YOUR MOTHER KNEW **TOO** MUCH--MORE THAN ANY MORTAL SHOULD ABOUT THE MAGIC REALM. AND AFTER THE WAR ENDED, AND YOUR FATHER WAS **DISCOVERED** TO BE A FOUR BLADES MEMBER AND KILLED, **SHE** WAS HUNTED DOWN BY THE CZARINA OF MEDIATION, **MEDINA**.

THE CZARINA OF MEDIATION!

YES, THE SAME POSITION HILDA NOW HOLDS. THE CZARINA OF MEDIATION'S JOB IS TO MAKE SURE THE MAGIC AND MORTAL REALMS REMAIN **SEPARATE**-- EVEN IF THAT MEANS THEY HAVE TO **WIPE** MEMORIES IN ORDER TO PROTECT PEOPLE!

YOU'RE TELLING ME THE CZARINA **ERASED** MY MOTHER'S MEMORY? YOU MEAN MY MOTHER **DIDN'T** ABANDON ME BECAUSE OF MY POWERS?

OF **COURSE** NOT! SHE LOVED YOU AND KNEW THAT YOU WERE A BUDDING WITCH!

BUT WHEN HER MEMORY WAS ERASED OF EVERYTHING RELATING TO MAGIC...SADLY... THAT INCLUDED **YOU**.

237

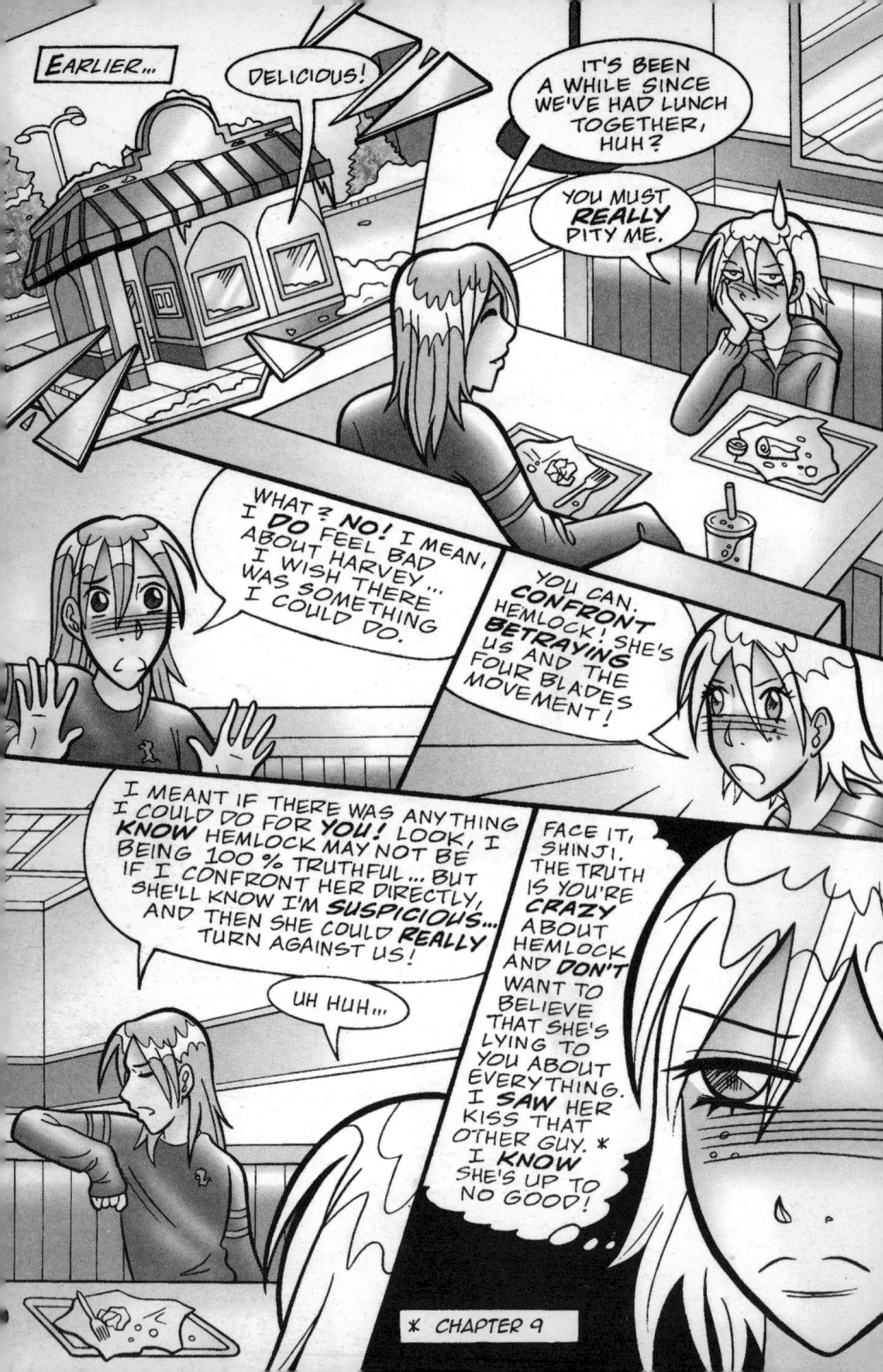

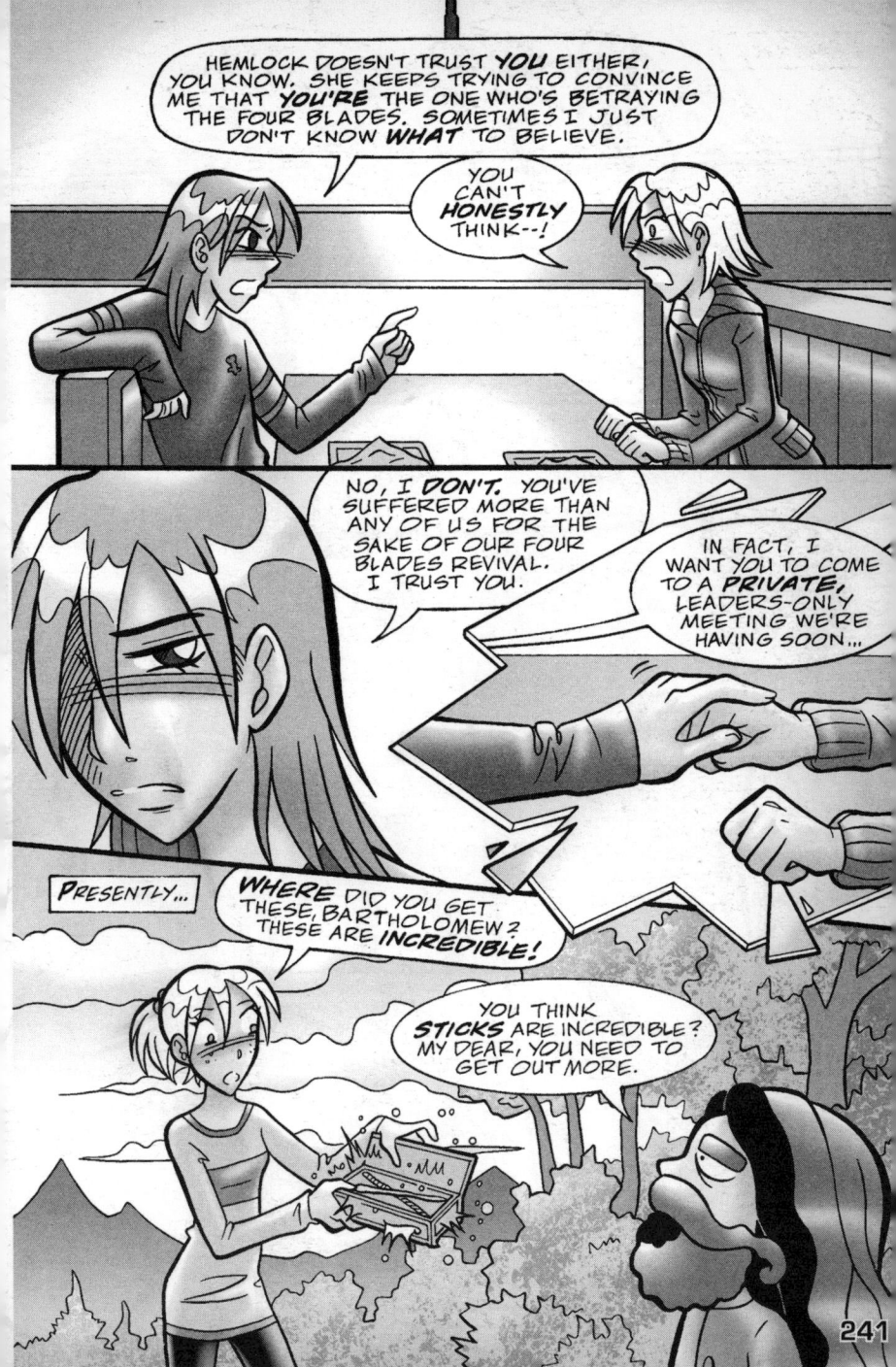

241

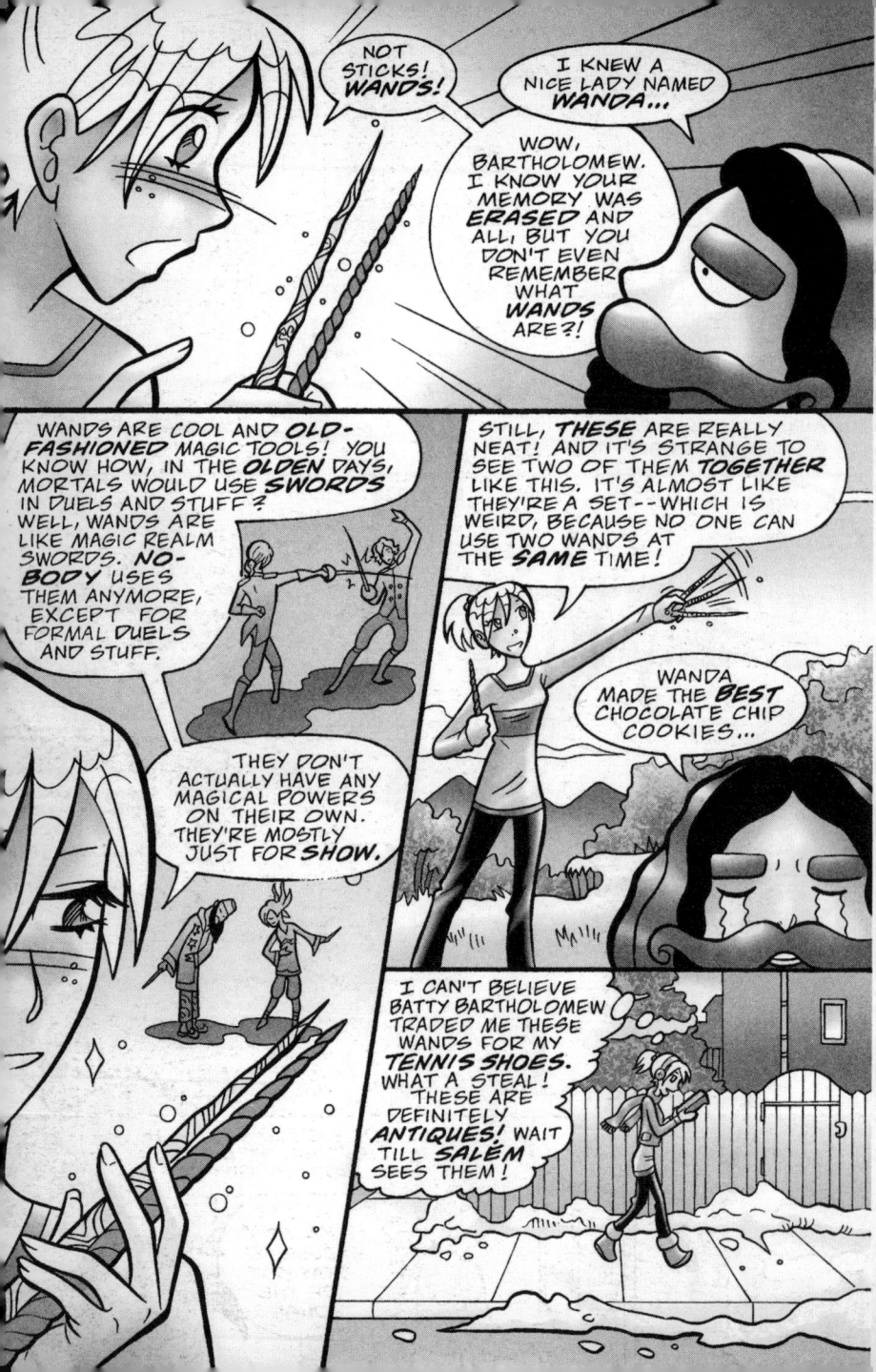

GWENEVIVE! HI!

I HEARD ABOUT HARVEY. I AM **SO** SORRY, 'BRINA. IT'S **TERRIBLE!**

I KNOW... I'VE BEEN TRYING TO SPEND AS MUCH TIME **DISTRACTING** MYSELF AS POSSIBLE. WANT TO COME UP AND HANG OUT FOR A WHILE?

I WOULD, BUT I HAVE TO **CHAPERONE** PUMPKIN'S **DATE** WITH SALEM!

D-**DATE**?! WITH SALEM? ARE WE TALKING ABOUT **MY** SALEM? THE RUDE, ANTI-SOCIAL CAT WHO LOVES HIS OWN **REFLECTION** MORE THAN ANYTHING ELSE?

YUP! YUP! HE'S CUTE **AND** SOFT LOOKING! AND IT ALWAYS LOOKS LIKE HE'S WEARING A **TUXEDO**, DOESN'T IT? HUH? HUH?

Shh! PUMPKIN! I TOLD YOU TO KEEP QUIET UNTIL WE'RE **AWAY** FROM THIS PLACE! AFTER WHAT HILDA DID TO HARVEY, I DON'T WANT TO TAKE ANY CHANCES.

I DON'T **BLAME** YOU...

WELL, LET ME RUN UP AND LET SALEM KNOW YOU'RE HERE.

YOU SHOULD COME **WITH** US, SABRINA. WE CAN TALK DURING THEIR DATE!

OK! I'LL TAKE **ANY** EXCUSE TO STAY OUT OF THE HOUSE!

245

MMM, THIS IS **REALLY** GOOD! SEEMS LIKE SALEM AND PUMPKIN ARE ENJOYING IT, TOO!

OPEN **WIDE**, SALEM!

SWEETHEART, IF THERE'S **ONE** THING I KNOW HOW TO DO ON MY OWN, IT'S FEED **MYSELF**.

THIS MEANS A **LOT** TO PUMPKIN. SHE'S SUCH A CHATTERBOX AND DOESN'T ALWAYS HAVE SOMEONE TO TALK TO. IT MUST BE **TOUGH** BEING THE **ONLY** MAGICAL DOG IN THE NEIGHBORHOOD! I FEEL **SORRY** FOR HER SOMETIMES.

I THINK HE **LIKES** BEING A CAT **MORE** THAN HE LIKED BEING HUMAN!

ALL THIS FOOD IS MAKING ME **SLEEPY**! I COULD **TOTALLY** GO FOR A NAP AFTER THIS...

I'D FEEL SORRY FOR SALEM TOO, BUT HE REALLY DOESN'T SEEM TO MIND SLEEPING AND EATING ALL DAY.

WELL, I DON'T **BLAME** HIM! I WOULDN'T MIND LAYING AROUND ALL DAY, EITHER. INSTEAD, I HAVE TO WORRY ABOUT WHAT I'M GOING TO DO AFTER I **GRADUATE**. IT'S KIND OF SCARY! YOU'RE LUCKY YOU STILL HAVE ONE MORE YEAR TO GO.

THEN WHY DON'T YOU GET A JOB IN THE **MAGIC REALM** AND MOVE THERE ONCE YOU GRADUATE?

YEAH, BUT AT LEAST YOU KNOW WHAT YOU'RE GOOD AT--**WRITING**. THE ONLY THING I'M GOOD AT IS **MAGIC**, AND THAT WON'T BE OF ANY HELP HERE.

MAYBE... BEFORE I WAS RELUCTANT TO LEAVE THE MORTAL REALM BECAUSE I DIDN'T WANT TO LEAVE **HARVEY** BEHIND,...BUT NOW...

DON'T TAKE THIS THE WRONG WAY... BUT MAYBE LOSING HARVEY WILL HELP YOU BECOME MORE *INDEPENDENT.* YOU CAN ACHIEVE WHAT-EVER YOU WANT, AND YOU DON'T HAVE TO WORRY ABOUT *HOLDING BACK* FOR HIS SAKE!

YOU DON'T UNDERSTAND... IT'S NOT *JUST* HARVEY. IT'S MY MORTAL *MOTHER.* SHE'S OUT THERE...SOMEWHERE. AND HER MEMORY WAS ERASED, TOO. EVERY-ONE I CARE MOST ABOUT CAN'T EVEN *REMEM-BER* WHO I AM. AND YOU COULD BE NEXT!

...

MMHPH MMM MPH!

THAT'S RIGHT! MORE *EATING,* LESS TALKING!..AS LONG AS YOU CAN REMEMBER THAT, I THINK WE'LL GET ALONG *JUUUST* FINE.

SLURP!

YOU GONNA FINISH THAT?

Now check out a sneak peek of what's next in
*Sabrina the Teenage Witch:
The Magic Within 4!*

To Be Continued!